We lovingly dedicate this book to our sons:

Gary, for his kind heart and commitment to protecting animals rights on our planet.

Brandon, a devoted, fun, and creative teacher, who understands the importance of compassion and human connection, inside and outside the classroom.

To all our sea friends and furry pals who make us smile!

Gizmo 4 President!

Publisher's note: This publication is designed, created, and sold with the understanding that the author, illustrator, and publisher are not engaged in rendering psychological or other professional services. If expert assistance or counseling is needed, the services of a competent professional should be sought.

ISBN 978-0-9992348-2-2

A heartfelt thank you to Jim Hunt for the creative illustrations and hand-lettering for the book. Jim brought Gizmo's imaginary world to life for our readers in his unique and spectacular cartoon sketches! Learn more about Jim's cartoon studio by visiting, www.JimHunt.us

A special thank you for the brilliant digital colors, book, and graphic design by Nisa Martinez.

Thank you to Vasi Siedman who captured the fun personality of Gizmo, along with the photos of Suzanne and Dulce. To see more of Vasi's furry friends, visit: www.PetPixAcademy.com

We are sending a huge thank you, along with "two paws up!" to our talented and creative editing team, Barbie Heit and Tina Peel.

Book font set in Mikado
First edition 2020

Proudly printed in the United States of America. Gizmo recognizes the individual and collective responsibilities of being good stewards for our environment. The happy people who print this book at Worzalla are certified FSC printers since 2008, who know that from the tree to paper, we publish our book on paper that is responsibly sourced.
www.Gizmo4President.com

"Grab your surfboard, put on your pup tux! Let's all surf the campaign trail!"

It was a beautiful sunny morning. The skies were blue, and the birds were chirping. Gizmo, stretched and yawned, ready to start the day. He opened his IPaw tablet to read the local news, as he did every morning.

But today, the headlines were not good! *The Surf Dog Daily* was reporting that a new canine **candidate** was running for **president**. The article said that Riley, a local surfer dog, was entering the presidential race.

It was not happy news for America since Riley was very unpopular at Tide Rider Beach. He was unkind to other surfers, and he did not have a good reputation for keeping the beach clean.

Gizmo was a surfer and a champion for keeping the beaches beautiful. There was nowhere Gizmo would rather be than on his surfboard, hanging ten while sharing waves with friends.

That afternoon, Gizmo met up with Professor Otty. His new pal was a wise college professor, but secretly, he wished to be an Olympic surfer.

News was spreading fast! Professor Otty had already heard that Riley was running for president.

"I have a great idea, Gizmo!" the professor said with confidence. "Why don't you run for president? I can't think of anyone that has more sea buddies than you. You could make a big difference for them by cleaning up the ocean!"

Gizmo felt a wave of inspiration from Professor Otty's words. Gizmo knew that pollution was hurting his sea friends.

"If I were president," he thought, "I would clean up the beaches and oceans to help the sea creatures smile again!"

Gizmo decided, then and there, to enter the canine presidential race. He knew it would be his mission to spread happiness and save the ocean.

Gizmo rushed to tell the news to Kaia, his best surfing pal.

Kaia thought Riley was a terrible choice for president. She reminded Gizmo how Riley had bullied them in the Puppy Cup Surfing Classic. Kaia was sure that Gizmo would be the best pup for president.

"Hey, Kaia, why don't you enter the race with me to help our sea friends?" cheered Gizmo.

Kaia agreed on the spot to campaign with Gizmo and become the vice-presidential candidate.

"Yes, together, we can make a difference for our sea friends!" said Kaia.

Soon, every newspaper reported the breaking news.

The day had come for Gizmo to stand face-to-face with Riley to announce his bid for canine president.

Riley could only sneer into the camera and say, "Gizmo is a silly surfer! The ocean is beautiful. Nothing needs to change."

Gizmo paused and took a few deep breaths. Remembering to breathe always helped him to focus during a challenging moment, like this one.

"I propose that coastal conservation is the most important thing for our future!" said Gizmo. "If we can clean and protect our oceans, I know we can help our sea-creature friends smile again!"

Riley quickly introduced Sammy Slick as his running mate. Sammy didn't have much to say. He just shook his head and agreed with everything Riley said.

Behind Gizmo's back, Riley reached for his phone and secretly sent out a message on social media:
"The ocean is beautiful just as it is, and Gizmo is a loser!"

His bully-like message and campaign slogan said it all:
Riley for Boss!

Gizmo didn't know how to begin something as big as the campaign for president. How could one little surfer pup reach so many, and inspire others to save the ocean?

"I know!" said Gizmo. "I will ask Professor Otty! He always has excellent advice."

"Gizmo, grab your board, put on your pup tux, and surf the campaign trail. It's as easy as riding a giant wave!" said the wise professor.

Again, Gizmo felt encouraged by Professor Otty's words. "Yes, I can do this!" said Gizmo confidently. "Yes, I can reach out to everyone, everywhere, one giant wave at a time!"

Gizmo and Kaia began the campaign at their favorite beach. The canine presidential race would be their most fun and crucial adventure ever!

"I have an idea," said Kaia. "*Surf With Me, Let's Save the Sea!* can be our campaign slogan."

"Yes, we can surf this!" cheered Gizmo.

At Tide Rider Beach and everywhere in America, Gizmo and Kaia shared their views about coastal conservation and the importance of saving marine life. They spoke about the need to clean up our waterways.

"Every drop of water from our rivers and streams ends up in the ocean. Let's all take action to save our seas!" said Gizmo.

Gizmo's campaign speech inspired Professor Otty.

The professor texted this message to Gizmo: "How about giving all the creatures a voice in this election? Let others help you. We can all work together and find ways to clean up the ocean and protect the environment."

Gizmo trusted the advice of his wise friend. He would consider all the ideas on how to take action.

CLICK CLICKETY CLICK

Gizmo was determined to let every creature have a voice in his campaign.

Across America, on land and sea, fantastic posters, photos, and videos were being shared to show ways to protect our environment. It was fast becoming a campaign of the heart.

Gizmo imagined what it would be like to be president! He thought about history's great leaders who surrounded themselves with trustworthy friends.

Gizmo remembered to dream big and believe he had all the support needed for his mission to succeed.

PRESIDENT GIZMO

Deep below the sea, Gizmo and his team
created a powerful wave of voices for change.

On land too, many others eagerly joined in Gizmo's campaign to help the sea creatures.

Riley wasn't interested in hitting the campaign trail. Most of the time, Riley could be spotted lounging at Tide Rider Beach. He scowled as he watched the crowd gather at Gizmo's campaign rally.

Riley sent out a social media message for everyone to see:

The next day, Gizmo went back to Professor Otty for support. "I'm having a rough time with Riley's mean messages." said Gizmo.

"Gizmo, don't give up. Remember, you're not alone," said the wise professor. "Don't let Riley's mean words distract you from your mission. Call on your supporters. Ask them to focus on caring about each other and our planet."

After the meeting with Professor Otty, Gizmo was more determined than ever to hit the campaign trail.

"Instead of complaining, let's listen and look for solutions. I see the ocean as our playground and everyone as a change-maker for the world!" cheered Gizmo.

The campaign was in full swing!

Popstar dolphins and fish formed rock bands to record upbeat songs to inspire compassion and awareness for marine conservation.

Music filled the air waves!

Across the country, crowds began listening to catchy tunes from deep below the sea. The musical messages inspired hearts and minds to help the sea creatures.

The news media reported about different groups taking action to clean up the environment. Many posted online messages about the importance of voting to save our oceans.

SAVE OUR SEAS!

RECYCLE!

Friends reminded friends that it was not cool to throw trash on the beach.

Many groups started to **recycle**, clean up the beach, and get rid of the plastic trash, and the straws that harm the sea turtles and marine life.

On land and in the sea, **committees** began to form. Their goal was to raise money for **budgets** to clean up the environment.

The clam committee eagerly worked together, being especially useful in **lobbying** for funding the cleanup!

Lawmakers introduced new laws and debated about budgets to save marine life.

They worked together to find solutions to help protect every living being and the planet's future.

The **elected officials** in every branch of government became examples of peace and co-operation.

News of Gizmo's coastal conservation
campaign began to spread to the entire world!

Everyone, in every country, remembered that
happiness begins with caring about our planet's future.

Election day had finally come!

Vast waves of voters came out to support Gizmo.
The election set a new record for voter turnout!

They knew that with Gizmo in charge,
things would continue to get better.

Gizmo won the election!

Gizmo celebrated all those who used their powerful voice
to vote for good things that help our planet!

The waves were cranking, and Gizmo's campaign team celebrated with him! Tide Rider Beach began to look **pristine** and sun-kissed.

GIZMO
HEADQUARTERS
4 PREZ

VOTE
FOR ME

35

Gizmo knew there was only one more important thing to do. Gizmo offered Riley his paw in friendship.

At first, Riley barked, "No Way!"

But then, as Riley thought more about it, he reached for Gizmo's paw. "I'm sorry for all the mean messages, Gizmo. I shouldn't have posted such mean words," said Riley.

Riley pitched in to clean up and discovered that he enjoyed the pristine beach, and when the sea creatures were smiling!

From that day on, Gizmo and Riley worked together as canine **ambassadors** for marine life.

As the sun went down, Gizmo and friends united to surf the gigantic wave of happiness across America!

Gizmo's Glossary of Cool Terms to Know

Ambassador – A representative who spreads a message to others.

Budget – A sum of money set aside for a specific purpose.

Campaign – A race between candidates for a position in government.

Candidate – Someone who is running for public office in government.

Champion – Someone who fights for a cause.

Coastal/Marine conservation – When groups work together to protect the plants and creatures in the waterways, oceans, and on the beaches.

Committees – A group appointed or elected to perform a specific duty.

Compassion – When we care about others, show kindness, and feel a strong desire to help those in need.

Debated – A discussion about an important topic and different views.

Elected official – Someone chosen by voters to be a government leader.

Hanging ten – A difficult stunt where a surfer rides out on the edge of a surfboard, curling his or her toes around it.

Kook – A surfer who thinks he or she is better than other surfers.

Lobbying – Working together in groups to inspire change in government.

Mission – A goal or plan to make something happen.

President – The highest elected official in the United States of America.

Vice-presidential candidate - Someone who is running for government office to work with and report directly to the president.

Pristine – Clean and pure.

Recycle – To turn items from the trash, such as glass, plastic, paper, or metal, into something useful again to reduce pollution.

Slogan – A short and powerful message.

Gizmo's Creative Campaign Team

Author

Suzanne Kline is a champion for volunteering with children's reading and literacy programs, actively promoting social-emotional learning initiatives in education.

She is the founder of The Surf's Up Gizmo Children's Foundation, Inc., a not-for-profit children's charity that actively provides no-cost books to underserved students in the schools. Suzanne is giving back by donating her book royalties to support the mission of www.SUGCFoundation.org.

Author/Publisher

Dulce Da Costa is a Florida-based family psychotherapist. She is a certified addictions professional and Clinical Hypnotherapist.

Dulce was born in Portugal and has traveled, lived, and worked in several European countries. She is proficient in Portuguese and Spanish.

Currently, Dulce resides in Florida with her zany, furry companions.

Gizmo/Presidential Candidate

Powered by a desire to clean up the oceans and save his sea buddies, Gizmo joins paws with his best pals in the canine presidential election.

Gizmo encourages kids to use their voices and to become ambassadors in protecting marine life.

Illustrator

Award-winning cartoonist Jim Hunt is the talented, professional illustrator who brings Gizmo, and other fun characters, to life in the story.

Jim currently resides in Philadelphia, PA, with his wife and their furry little art director, Sofia. Learn more about Jim's cartoon studio by visiting: www.JimHunt.us

Graphic Designer

Nisa Martinez is the graphic artist behind the scenes who designed the book layout, along with the brilliant digital colors.

A love for compelling storytelling inspires her to imagine Gizmo's world in a fun and unique way.

At home with her family, Nisa enjoys spending time with her two long-haired dachshunds who always manage to brighten her day!